THE
READ-ALOUD
STORYBOOK

FOR YOUNG CHILDREN

Joyce Dunbar

Illustrated by
Colin & Moira Maclean

Kingfisher Books

NEW YORK

KINGFISHER BOOKS
Grisewood & Dempsey Inc.
95 Madison Avenue, New York, New York 10016

First American edition 1993
2 4 6 8 10 9 7 5 3 1

Library of Congress Cataloging-in-Publication Data
Dunbar, Joyce.
Read-aloud storybook / Joyce Dunbar, Moira & Colin Maclean.   1st American ed.
p. cm.
At head of title: Kingfisher.
Summary: A collection of new and traditional stories, including
"Tom Thumb," "The Sea Dragon," "Lazy Jack," and "Fighty-Bitey."
1. Children's stories.   2. Tales.   [1. Short stories.   2. Fairy
tales.   3. Folklore.]   I. Maclean, Moira, ill.   II. Maclean, Colin,
1930– , ill.   III. Title.   IV. Title: Kingfisher read-aloud
storybook.
PZ5.D866Re   1993
[E]–dc20   92-29125   CIP   AC

ISBN 1-85697-911-3

Edited by Caroline Walsh
Designed by Caroline Johnson

Printed in Hong Kong

CONTENTS

THE WONDER BROOM *Traditional* 4

THE THREE WISHES *The Brothers Grimm* 10

THE WALKING FLOWER *Jenny Koralek* 15

PEBBLE-DASH PIE *Traditional Czech* 22

THE SEA DRAGON *James Mayhew* 27

THE OLD WOMAN AND HER PIG *Traditional* 31

THE BRAVEST CAT IN THE WORLD *Ann Turnbull* 38

LAZY JACK *Traditional* 45

FIGHTY-BITEY *Andrew Davies* 52

THE WISE GUY *Traditional African* 56

RHODA RED-HEN *Caroline Pitcher* 60

THE BRIC-A-BRACS *Joyce Dunbar* 69

TOM THUMB *Traditional* 75

THE WONDER BROOM

Traditional

Philipippa was the kitchen maid in King Carraway's palace. She washed the Royal Dishes, peeled the Royal Potatoes, and swept the Royal Floors.

She did a lot more work besides, for the Royal Cook was a bully who never stopped bossing her around.

The Royal Cook was also very fat. Her cotton print dresses were so tight that it looked as if the buttons might burst at any moment.

One morning, the Royal Cook sent Philipippa to market to buy a new broom. "This old one is disgusting, a disgrace to the Royal Household," she said crossly.

"Yes, Ma'am," Philipippa answered politely.

4

It didn't take Philipippa long to get to market. She tried every stall but she couldn't find a broom anywhere. She didn't dare go back to the Royal Palace without one, for then the cook's buttons would surely burst.

She was wondering what to do when a peddler came by. "Wonder brooms! Wonder brooms!" he shouted.

"But you have only one broom," said Philipippa.

"Why yes. These brooms are so wonderful that I have sold all the others," lied the peddler. "This is the last one left." He didn't tell her that he had found just that one broom on the Royal Road that very morning!

Philipippa bought the wonder broom and hurried back to the Royal Palace.

"Dawdler! What a time you've been!" the cook scolded.

"Indeed, Ma'am, I—"

"Enough of your rudeness!" snapped the cook. "And don't just stand there gawking. Anybody would think we had nothing to do! I've been making the stuffing for the Royal Goose and the crumbs have gone all over the floor. Sweep the kitchen! Sweep the hall! Sweep the yard!" With that, the cook snatched up a Royal Saucepan and banged it down on the fire so hard that hot coals shot off in all directions.

"My! What a temper she has," thought Philipippa, nervously watching out for buttons.

She picked up the new broom and began sweeping the floor. Over the Royal Red Tiles flew the wonder broom, swish, swish, swish. She had no sooner begun than it was done. Not a crumb nor a hot coal in sight! Philipippa

stared in amazement. It really was a wonder broom. So light! It must be enchanted.

"Well, if this isn't my lucky day," said Philipippa, patting the broom affectionately. "We are going to be great friends, I can see."

Next day, quite early, a crotchety old woman came knocking on the Royal Kitchen door. Philipippa had almost finished all her sweeping for the morning so the cook was about to set her scrubbing. But first she had to answer the door.

"May I ask what you are doing with my broom," snapped the crotchety old woman.

"*Your* broom?" cried Philipippa in astonishment. "Why, I bought it myself in the market yesterday."

"What if you did?" said the crotchety old woman. "I tell you it is *my* broom, just the same," and she tried to snatch it away.

"Well, and what about me?" the broom asked suddenly, in a swishy, swooshy voice.

Philipippa was so surprised that she let go of the broom handle with a jerk. It didn't fall, but stood all by itself in the middle of the floor!

"Come here at once!" cackled the crotchety old woman. "How *dare* you run away like that?"

"Run away yourself," piped the broom, "you crusty old cross-patch. I am much happier where I am, thank you."

"Oh, are you?" cried the old woman. "We'll soon see who's the boss around here."

"Oh, shall we?" retorted the broom, quivering with rage.

"Go away at once or I'll sweep you out!"

"Oh, you mustn't do that," said Philipippa.

But no sooner had she spoken than the broom began sweeping as hard as it could go. It swept the old woman out of the kitchen, across the courtyard and over the palace drawbridge. Swish, swish, swish!

The cook came running to see what was the matter.

Swish, swish, swish, went the broom! Pop, pop, pop, went the cook's buttons! She burst right out of her dress and went running away in her petticoat.

And then all of a sudden the broom was back in Philipippa's hand, just as if nothing had happened.

The cook and the crotchety old woman didn't come back, so Philipippa kept the wonder broom. And though she never told anyone the tale, no one ever bullied her again!

THE THREE WISHES

The Brothers Grimm

There was once a poor man who had a very pretty wife. They were so poor that they had hardly enough to eat and hardly enough wood to make a fire. But one winter evening, the man came in with a shiny brass coal scuttle, piled high with coal. "Look what I found by the door," he said to his wife. "It must be a gift. We shall have a good blaze tonight."

They sat down to warm themselves and the wife began to talk about the neighbors. "They are happier than we are because they are richer," said the wife. "But if only we could meet a fairy, who would grant us a wish, we should be happier and richer than all of them."

"That would be a fine thing," said her husband.

No sooner had they spoken than a fairy fell from the embers of the glowing fire.

"I will grant you a wish," said the fairy.

"Three would be better," said the wife.

"Very well then," said the fairy. "Three wishes. But *only* three wishes. I will grant you nothing more." And with that, she faded away.

The man and his wife settled down to decide what to wish for. "I will not make a wish yet," said the wife, "but I think nothing could be better than an embroidered silk purse, full of gold."

"What a silly wish," said her husband. "Why, you could wish for ten silk purses, twenty, or even a hundred. But what use would they be to you if you were sick? It would be much better to wish for health, happiness, and a long life."

"But what is the use of a long life if you are poor? It only makes the misery last longer. Now I come to think of it, that fairy should have granted us a dozen wishes. Then we could have everything we want."

"That's true," said her husband. "But never mind. If we take our time and think carefully, we will make the most of our three wishes."

"I will think all night and make my mind up in the morning," said his wife. "Meanwhile, let us warm ourselves by the fire, for it is very cold." She poked the fire until it flared up very nicely, but her stomach rumbled with hunger. "Ah," she sighed, without thinking.

"What a splendid fire. I wish we had a length of sausage to cook on it for our supper."

She had hardly said these words when clitter-clatter down the chimney came a length of sausage, more than enough for two.

Her husband was furious. "You greedy guts!" he shouted. "You and your sausage! What a waste of a good wish! Why, I wish that ridiculous sausage was fastened to the end of your nose!"

He soon felt sorry he had spoken, for the sausage jumped up immediately and stuck fast on the end of his pretty wife's nose.

"Owwww! What have you done to me?" wailed the wife. "Get it off!"

Her husband gave it a pull but it stuck. She gave it a

pull but it stuck. They both pulled so hard that they nearly pulled her nose off, but it was really, really stuck.

"I'm sorry, wife," said the husband. "But what if I were to wish for that embroidered silk purse, after all? You could use it to hide the sausage."

"Owwww!" wailed the wife. "I should hide my head in that coal scuttle. How could I bear to be seen with a sausage dangling from the end of my nose, even with a silk purse to hide it? Oh, I do wish it would drop off."

That very instant, the sausage dropped off the wife's nose and fell to the floor.

"There goes our last wish," groaned her husband.

"Owwww! Owwww! Owwww!" wailed the wife.

But she sat down and thought for a while, until at last she came to her senses. "It serves us right. We asked for too

much and this is how the fairy has punished us. From now on we should count our blessings. See! We have a shiny brass coal scuttle half full of coal. We have a sausage. That is more than we had to begin with. Why don't we sit here by the warm fire and cook this delicious sausage for our supper?"

And they did. And oh, it was good.

THE WALKING FLOWER

Jenny Koralek

Last time Rose and Harry spent the day with Grandma everything went wrong before it went right.

Rose was clack-clacking round the kitchen in Grandma's shoes, doing a dance she had just made up.

Harry was sitting under the table, clutching the shiny apple Grandma had given him, to stop him whining about missing Mom.

Grandma's rear was sticking out of the closet where she was looking for her shopping bag.

And the cat was on the mat, rolling and stretching his jaws, his paws, and his claws . . . *when:*

15

Harry bit hugely into his apple and . . . a wobbly tooth
fell out . . .

Grandma bonked her nose on the mop handle *and* . . .

Rose tripped over the cat and fell crashing to the floor.

PANDEMONIUM!

"Ow!" said Harry.

"Ouch!" said Grandma.

"OOOAAAOWWWCH!" yelled Rose. "My foot! My
foot! It hurts! I can't walk!"

Harry and Grandma lifted Rose onto a bed of chairs and
soft fat cushions and then they took Rose's shoe off.

Her foot was swelling up fast and Rose began to cry and
to be cross.

"Silly cat," sobbed Rose. "He shouldn't lie on the mat when I'm dancing . . ."

"Don't cry, Rose," said Harry. "You can put my tooth under your pillow and have the tooth fairy's money . . ."

"There isn't any tooth fairy," snapped Rose.

"Oh yes, there is," said Harry.

"Oh no, there isn't," said Rose.

"Now, now, you two!" said Grandma. "We still have to go shopping for our dinner and some ice cream. We'll just have to put you into Harry's old stroller for our quick trip up to the store."

"I'm *much* too big to go in a stroller," growled Rose.

"Then we'll stay here," said Grandma, "and not have any dinner and . . . no ice cream."

"Ohh, put me in the stroller then," said Rose. "But I will choose the ice cream and have three helpings."

"Hmm," said Grandma, "we'll see. We'll see . . ."

And she went back to the closet and pulled out the stroller left over from Harry's toddling days.

Harry felt sorry for Rose. He wished he could give her a bunch of flowers like Dad sometimes gave to Mom, or if not a whole bunch, just one really lovely flower.

Grandma pushed Rose through the park while Harry dawdled behind them staring at the flowers, red, white, and blue, standing in straight rows like soldiers.

"Shall we play a game, like I See Something . . . ?" said Grandma to Rose.

"No," said Rose.

"Don't be rude," said Grandma, "and hurry up, Harry.

You know you mustn't pick those flowers."

In the market Grandma bought potatoes, fresh peas, three shiny silver fish, and three rosy peaches.

"Shall I put some ice on your sore foot?" said the man at the fish stand.

"No," said Rose.

"Come on, cross-patch!" said the man at the fruit stand. "Give us a smile!"

"No," said Rose.

"Don't be so rude," said Grandma. "I know your foot hurts, I know you don't like sitting in Harry's stroller, but don't be so rude."

There were hundreds of flowers in the market, small ones,

tall ones, all the colors of the rainbow, but Harry had no money and he didn't want to ask Grandma for some. He wanted to find some flowers for Rose all by himself — but how and where?

"Come on, Harry!" called Grandma. "What a dawdler, what a dreamer you are today."

She took Rose into the corner store to buy some cat food.

Harry had one foot into the store when out of the corner of his eye he saw . . . the flower.

It was growing in an empty place next to the shop, a place where old tin cans and bottles lay among the weeds.

It was a yellow flower.

19

A giant flower.

A sunflower with a bumblebee buzzing in its dark brown heart.

Harry looked up at the sunflower.

"This is the right one for Rose," he said to himself and he began tugging and tugging at the flower's thick stalk.

He tugged and tugged until — at last! — up came the flower, roots and all, up out of the dark brown earth.

The bumblebee buzzed off and Grandma and Rose came out of the shop. Rose was still looking very cross.

"Where's Harry?" said Grandma. "Harry!" she called. "Where are you?"

Up the street came a giant walking flower.

"Well!" said Grandma. "A walking flower! That's something I've never seen in all my born days. *But . . . where is Harry?*"

Harry peeped out from behind the sunflower.

"Here you are, Rose," he said. "Here is a flower . . . specially for you . . . to make you feel better."

And then, at last, Rose smiled.

"You can choose the ice cream, Harry," she said.

"Now that," said Grandma, "is a very good idea . . . and we will *all* have three helpings and then," she smiled at Harry, "I'll take you home to Mom. . . . "

PEBBLE-DASH PIE

Traditional Czech

One dark night, a traveler was trudging through the snow. He was cold and hungry, so he knocked on the door of a cottage near the road.

"May I come in and shelter?" he called.

An old woman shuffled to the door.

"All right," she said gruffly, "but you'd better be off in the morning." She hated to give something for nothing.

"Can you spare me a little food to eat?" the traveler asked.

"Oh dear," the old woman sighed. "I haven't a scrap of

food in the house. I haven't eaten myself since yesterday. It's terrible to be so poor."

"I know just what you mean," said the traveler.

He sat down and sniffed the air once or twice. Then with an odd little smile, he took a pebble out of his pocket and rubbed it on his jacket.

"As you are so poor, I suppose I could rustle up a pebble-dash pie for us to share."

The old woman gaped at him.

"Pebble-dash pie? I've never heard of such a thing," she said, looking curiously at the pebble. "But I'll have some all the same." She loved to get something for nothing.

"Good," said the traveler. "Just bring me a large pot and some water."

The old woman scuttled away and found a large pot which she filled up with water. The traveler put it on the stove and dropped in the pebble. The old woman's eyes

almost popped out of her head when the traveler started to stir the mixture with a long spoon.

"Mmmm," he said. "This smells delicious. Would you like to taste it?"

"No, thank you," said the old woman, "for I'm sure it needs salt and pepper."

"If you say so," said the traveler. "Just a dash."

So the old woman brought salt and pepper and the traveler sprinkled some into the pot. The traveler sniffed and stirred.

"Mmmmmm. Much better," he said. "Would you like to taste it now?"

"No, thank you," said the old woman, "for I'm sure it needs a bit of onion."

"If you say so," said the traveler. "Just a dash."

The old woman brought a big fat onion and the traveler chopped it up into the pot. He sniffed and stirred some more.

"You *are* a good cook," he said to the old woman. "It smells much better now. Here. Have a taste."

"No, thank you," said the old woman, "for I'm sure it could do with some carrots and potatoes."

"If you say so," said the traveler. "Just a dash."

So the old woman peeled carrots and potatoes and dropped them into the pot. The traveler went on sniffing and stirring.

"Nearly, nearly ready!" he said, hungrily licking his lips.

"Are you sure it doesn't need some meat?" asked the old woman.

"If you say so," said the traveler. "Just a dash."

Once more, the old woman hurried off to the pantry and this time she came back with some meat.

"Mmmmarvelous!" said the traveler. "This pie will be fit for a king."

"Pie?" said the old woman. "How can you call it a pie? You need pastry to make a pie."

"So you do," said the traveler. "How stupid of me. And you need a pie dish, too."

So the old woman rolled out some pastry while the traveler poured the mixture into a pie dish. Then they put it in the oven to cook.

By now it was really smelling good and the old woman

was as hungry as the traveler. When it was ready she dished it out onto two plates. They had the most wonderful meal in front of the fire and the old woman could not praise the pie enough.

"Who would believe it?" she said. "A pie, made with a pebble!"

The traveler mopped up his gravy, leaving a small pebble on the side of his plate.

"It is the best pebble-dash pie I have ever made," he said. "And it is all thanks to your good advice. In return, I will give you this pebble. Now you can make pebble-dash pie whenever you like."

"Why, thank you," said the old woman, for she loved to get something for nothing!

THE SEA DRAGON

James Mayhew

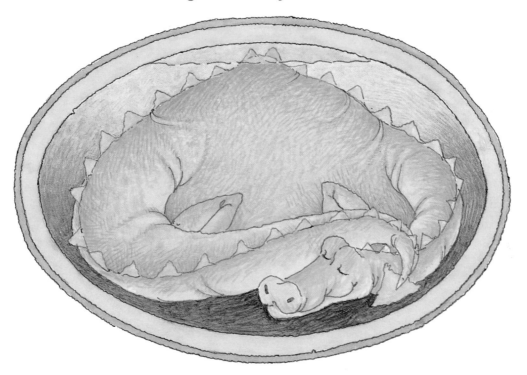

Right out at sea, I'm not saying where exactly, lives the sea dragon. He is enormous, and can eat up a whole country at a time. When he rolls over, mountains shake and crumble, and waves the size of houses crash onto the shore. But mostly, the sea dragon just sleeps; he is like a cat after a big dinner — fat and lazy.

Once, the sea dragon ate a great big country with snow-capped mountains and thick forests. It was very tasty, for the sea dragon was fond of crunchy forests and scrunchy snowy mountains. Then he curled up on the ocean's bed for a nice long sleep.

And what a long sleep it was! Not for hours or days did he sleep, but for weeks, months, and years! And yet, all the time he did not realize that his blanket, the sea, had not tucked him in properly, so that a small part of his knobbly, spiky back stuck out of the water.

Then rain fell upon the sea dragon's back. The sun shone

too, and after a few years, a forest started to grow. Snow fell onto the mountainous spikes. Birds nested there. Animals swam there to live. But they were no trouble at all, so the sea dragon didn't notice them, and slept on.

Soon his back was a beautiful green island, and it wasn't much longer before a discoverer sailed past on a ship.

"My goodness, that would make a good place to live," said the discoverer, and he sailed back to his own country

28

to tell everyone about the beautiful green island.

"No more crowds," he said to some people.

"No more noise," he told the others.

"No more dirt and grime," he said to them all.

All the people packed their suitcases and sailed to the island. They all agreed that it was a beautiful place to live,

and they thanked the explorer for finding such a lovely country for them.

The years passed and still the sea dragon slept. Everyone built houses, and they made roads so that everyone could visit everyone else. And when those jobs were done, the people built factories and machines, and dug deep, deep holes into the ground to find precious stones and gold.

The animals soon got fed up and they swam away.

But the sea dragon slept on.

The people cut down the forest, because it took up too much room. They dug up the green grass, they drilled holes in the mountains to make tunnels. The birds got scared and so they flew away.

They made so much noise and so much nuisance that, at last, the sea dragon woke up.

First he opened one giant eye. Then he opened another great big eye. Then he said:

"How my back itches!" He scratched himself, and rolled right over before going back to sleep.

A little piece of his back was still sticking out of the sea, but now there was nothing on it at all.

THE OLD WOMAN
AND HER PIG

Traditional

An old woman was sweeping her house when she found a crooked sixpence. "What shall I do with this sixpence?" she said. "I know, I will go to market and buy a pig."

Then the old woman went to the market and bought a pig. On her way home she came to a stile but the pig would not go over the stile.

"Pig, pig, get over the stile," she said,

"or I cannot get home tonight."

But the pig would not.

She went a little farther and met a dog; and she said to the dog:

"Dog, dog, bite pig.

Pig won't get over the stile and I cannot get home tonight."

But the dog would not.

She went a little farther and met a stick; and she said to the stick:

"Stick, stick, beat dog.

Dog won't bite pig.

Pig won't get over the stile and I cannot get home tonight."

But the stick would not.

She went a little farther and met a fire; and she said to the fire:

"Fire, fire, burn stick.

Stick won't beat dog.

Dog won't bite pig.

Pig won't get over the stile and I cannot get home tonight."

But the fire would not.

She went a little farther and met some water; and she said to the water:

"Water, water, quench fire.

Fire won't burn stick.

Stick won't beat dog.

Dog won't bite pig.

Pig won't get over the stile and I cannot get home tonight."

But the water would not.

She went a little farther and met an ox; and she said to the ox:

"Ox, ox, drink water.

Water won't quench fire.

Fire won't burn stick.

Stick won't beat dog.

Dog won't bite pig.

Pig won't get over the stile and I cannot get home tonight."

But the ox would not.

She went a little farther and met a butcher; and she said to the butcher:

"Butcher, butcher, tie ox.

Ox won't drink water.

Water won't quench fire.

Fire won't burn stick.

Stick won't beat dog.

Dog won't bite pig.

Pig won't get over the stile and I cannot get home tonight."

But the butcher would not.

She went a little farther and met a rope; and she said to the rope:

"Rope, rope, whip butcher.

Butcher won't tie ox.

Ox won't drink water.

Water won't quench fire.

Fire won't burn stick.

Stick won't beat dog.

Dog won't bite pig.

Pig won't get over the stile and I cannot get home tonight."

But the rope would not.

She went a little farther and met a rat; and she said to the rat:

"Rat, rat, gnaw rope.

Rope won't whip butcher.

Butcher won't tie ox.

Ox won't drink water.

Water won't quench fire.

Fire won't burn stick.

Stick won't beat dog.

Dog won't bite pig.

Pig won't get over the stile and I cannot get home tonight."

But the rat would not.

She went a little farther and met a cat; and she said to the cat:

"Cat, cat, chase rat.

Rat won't gnaw rope.

Rope won't whip butcher.

Butcher won't tie ox.

Ox won't drink water.

Water won't quench fire.

Fire won't burn stick.

Stick won't beat dog.

Dog won't bite pig.

Pig won't get over the stile and I cannot get home tonight."

But the cat said to her: "If you will go to yonder cow and fetch me a saucer of milk, I will chase the rat." So away went the old woman to the cow.

But the cow said to her: "If you will go to yonder haystack and fetch me a handful of hay, I will give you some milk." So away went the old woman to the haystack and brought some hay for the cow.

As soon as the cow had eaten the hay, she gave the old woman the milk. As soon as the old woman had the milk she gave it in a saucer to the cat. As soon as the cat saw the milk she lapped it all up. Then:

The cat began to chase the rat; the rat began to gnaw the rope; the rope began to whip the butcher; the butcher began to tie the ox; the ox began to drink the water; the water began to quench the fire; the fire began to burn the stick; the stick began to beat the dog; the dog began to bite the pig; the pig gave a loud squeal and got over the stile and the old woman got home that night.

THE BRAVEST CAT
IN THE WORLD

Ann Turnbull

Little Cat was brave. He said so. He said, "I am the bravest cat in the world. I chase mice. I chase butterflies. I chase sparrows and beetles and gnats and bees. Everything in the garden is afraid of me."

Big Cat was basking in the sun. He yawned a pink yawn. He said, "You're not brave. You're just a bully. One of these days something will frighten you."

"Not me!" said Little Cat.

But he had run out of things to chase.

"I'm going next door," he said.

"Watch out for the dog," said Big Cat.

Little Cat squeezed through the hedge into the yard next door.

He heard barking.

A dog bounded out from behind a bush.

Little Cat ran. The dog leaped after him, but he was tied up; the rope stopped his spring. He barked and strained at the rope.

Little Cat felt braver. He crept close to the dog until he was just out of reach. Then he arched his back and hissed.

The dog barked and barked, but he couldn't catch Little Cat. Little Cat hissed again and went home.

"I am the bravest cat in the world," he told Big Cat. "I frightened the dog."

Big Cat caught the tip of his tail between his paws and licked it clean. "One of these days," he said, "something will frighten you."

"Not me!" said Little Cat. "I'm going two doors down."

"Watch out for the rooster," said Big Cat.

Little Cat jumped over the wall and into the yard two doors down. He saw hens. He stalked them, swishing his tail. The hens flapped and squawked and scolded.

The rooster marched out from behind the henhouse.

Little Cat ran. The rooster followed him. Little Cat saw

the rooster's stabbing beak and curved claws. He climbed
a tree.

Now he felt braver. He arched his back and hissed.

The cockercl paced up and down under the tree but he
couldn't catch Little Cat.

Little Cat hissed again and went home.

"I am the bravest cat in the world," he told Big Cat. "I
frightened the rooster."

Big Cat licked his left paw and whisked it around his ears.
"One of these days," he said, "something will frighten you."

"Not me!" said Little Cat. "I'm going three doors down."

"Watch out for the pigeons," said Big Cat.

Little Cat slipped through a hole in the fence into the yard three doors down. He saw the pigeon loft. He heard the pigeons. "Croo-oom, croo-oom," they said.

Little Cat saw pigeons flying down. There was a ledge high on the side of the loft. One by one the pigeons landed on it and slipped inside through a gap. Little Cat hid in the grass and watched.

"Croo-oom, croo-oom," said the pigeons from inside the loft. Little Cat crept out of his hiding place. He ran to the loft and climbed up.

The gap was bird-sized. Little Cat peered in. He saw feathers and beaks and eyes. He heard flutterings and rustlings. His tail began to twitch.

He made himself small. He became a mere sliver of a cat. He squeezed through — and tumbled down onto the floor of the loft.

At once there was an explosion of wings. Wings beat like thunder; feathers brushed his face; beaks and claws and angry eyes swept by.

"Meow!" cried Little Cat. "Let me out!"

He looked for the way out. It was high up, and the loft was full of frantic pigeons. Pigeons swooped down beating him with their wings. Little Cat was knocked to the ground.

"Meow! Meow!" he cried.

He looked up and saw the ledge. He leaped at the wall, clinging with his claws. Wings beat and battered him; feathers flew. Little Cat fell to the floor in a storm of wings.

"Meow!" he cried. "Big Cat! Save me! Meow! Meow!"

Big Cat couldn't hear him. But someone else did. A door

opened. Little Cat saw shoes and a broom and heard a man's voice. The broom prodded him. It pushed him out of the door, out into fresh air and safety.

Little Cat ran. He ran across lawns, across flowerbeds, through the hole in the fence, over the wall, under the hedge; he ran all the way to his own yard and sprang through his own cat-flap.

Big Cat was cleaning his whiskers. He saw Little Cat's bristling fur and wide-open eyes. He guessed that Little

Cat would not visit the pigeons again.

"It's a fine evening," he said. "What will you be chasing tonight, Little Cat?"

Little Cat lay down and stretched. He examined his claws like a cat who has hunted well.

"I've had a busy day," he said. "Tonight I think I shall rest."

LAZY JACK

Traditional

There was once a boy named Jack who lived with his mother in a tiny cottage. They were very poor and Jack's mother had to work hard every day, chopping up carrots for dinner. But Jack did no work at all. In summer he lazed in the sun. In winter he loafed by the fire. Everyone called him Lazy Jack.

At last, one Monday morning, Jack's mother decided that enough was enough. "Jack," she said to her son, "You must go out and earn some money or there will be nothing for supper but carrots, carrots, and more carrots!"

Now Jack had also decided that enough was enough—
and he'd had more than enough carrots. So he went out
and got himself a gardening job. He spent a whole day
weeding and clipping and was given only a few small
coins for his pains. But Jack wasn't used to having money
and he accidentally dropped it in the river on his way home.

"Dear oh dear," said his mother. "You should have put
the money in your pocket."

"I hadn't thought of that," said Jack.

On Tuesday, Jack got some work with a farmer, looking
after the cows. At the end of the day he was given a jug
of milk to take home.

Remembering what his mother had said, Jack put the
jug of milk in the large pocket of his jacket, spilling it all
the way home.

"You silly boy," said his mother. "You should have carried it on your head."

"I never thought of that," said Jack.

Well, the next day was Wednesday and Jack got work in the dairy, helping to churn the butter. At the end of the day he was given a large pat of butter to take home.

Even though the sun was hot, Jack followed his mother's advice and put the pat of butter on his head. By the time he got home the butter had melted, running down his face and down his neck and all over him.

"You stupid idiot," said his mother. "You should have wrapped it up and carried it carefully in your hands."

"I didn't think of that," said Jack.

Thursday came and Jack got work with a baker, helping to bake the bread. But at the end of the day he was given

nothing but a large tomcat for his trouble.

Jack thought this was a pity. It would have been easy to wrap up a loaf of bread and carry it home in his hands. But when he tried to wrap up the tomcat, it scratched him so much that he was forced to let it go.

"You nincompoop," said his mother. "You should have put it on a string and pulled it along after you."

"So I should," said Jack.

Friday was Jack's lucky day. He managed to get work with a butcher who rewarded him with a large leg of lamb. "This will make a wonderful supper," thought Jack, tying the lamb with string and dragging it home in the dirt. Of course, the meat was completely spoiled.

"You great booby!" said his mother, really losing her
temper. "We've had nothing but carrots to eat for a week
and for the weekend we've only got cabbage! You should
have put the leg of lamb on your shoulder."

"I really will try to remember," said Jack.

On Saturday, Jack got work cleaning out some stables. At
the end of the day he was given a donkey as payment.

Although the donkey was very heavy, Jack was deter-
mined to do what his mother had said, and he hoisted the
donkey onto his shoulders. Then he began to stagger
home proudly with his prize.

Now it so happened that on the way he had to pass by a
house where a rich man lived with his beautiful deaf

49

daughter, who had never laughed nor spoken. She was looking out of the window when Jack passed by, carrying the donkey on his shoulders.

The poor beast was kicking its legs in the air and hee-hawing with all its might. The deaf girl had never seen anything so funny in all her life and she immediately burst out laughing. She laughed so much and so loud that she discovered that she had a voice, and for the first time, she tried to speak.

Her father was overjoyed and invited Jack and his mother to Sunday dinner next day. They had roast beef, green beans, roast potatoes, and gravy, followed by apple pie and cream.

Jack fell in love with the rich man's daughter and she fell in love with him. They were married and Jack's mother never had to work again. And shall I tell you what they never had for supper?

Carrots! They had no more carrots!

FIGHTY-BITEY

Andrew Davies

Megan was a very nice young dog, but she could be a bit excitable. She lived in a house with some people called Mr. Green and Mrs. Green, and Nicola Green, who were very fond of her, and a cat called Kevin. Kevin was not very fond of Megan, because sometimes when she was extra hungry she would eat his dinner as well as her own, and sometimes when she was feeling playful she would chase him upstairs. Kevin, who was rather a fat cat, hated being chased.

One day, Mrs. Green looked at the calendar and said: "Nicola! It's Megan's birthday tomorrow! What shall we do about it?"

"I know," said Nicola. "Let's invite Kim and Emma and have a party."

"Hmmm," said Mrs. Green. "Not too sure about that."

"Please, Mom," said Nicola. "We'll be good."

"Well," said Mrs. Green. "It *is* her birthday. All right, you can invite them."

Kim was Nicola's best friend, and Emma was Megan's best friend. Emma was a bit excitable, too. But it *was* Megan's birthday, and she *did* love having her friend over.

So Kim and Emma came to Megan's birthday party.

Nicola and Kim played with Nicola's toys, and Megan and Emma played with each other.

First they played in the yard. They played roly-poly wrestling (unfortunately some flowers got squashed) and then they played Pull the Washing Off the Line (unfortunately all the family's clean clothes got muddy).

Mr. and Mrs. Green came out and shouted at them, so they went in the house and played Fighty-Bitey (as they were best friends they only pretended to bite each other). They enjoyed playing Fighty-Bitey very much, but unfortunately a vase of flowers got knocked over and somehow the sofa got covered with muddy paw prints.

"Megan! Emma! You bad dogs!" said Nicola and Kim. Megan and Emma were very sorry and wagged their tails and promised to be good. But just then, Kevin came in. "Hello, Kev!" barked Emma. "Let's play Chasey-Chasey!"

Kevin was so alarmed that he jumped straight up the chimney, and Mr. Green had to get a ladder and rescue him from the roof.

Then it was suppertime. The two friends were quiet for three whole minutes while they had their supper.

After supper, Nicola and Kim left Megan and Emma in the kitchen to have a rest. This was a mistake, because Megan and Emma weren't tired yet. Emma, who was a very clever dog, showed Megan some tricks. She showed her how to tip trash out of trash bins, and how to open closet doors, and how to open refrigerators. Then she showed Megan a new game called Tug-of-War With Sausages. When they had finished playing Tug-of-War With Sausages, the two friends were very tired and they lay down for a nap.

After a while Mr. and Mrs. Green and Nicola and Kim tiptoed into the kitchen.

"I think it's time for Emma to go home," said Mr. Green.

Mr. and Mrs. Green and Nicola and Megan watched Kim and Emma get into the car.

"Mom," said Nicola. "It's nice to have your best friend to a party when it's your birthday, isn't it?"

"Hmmm," said Mrs. Green.

THE WISE GUY

Traditional African

There were two men who had been the best of friends since childhood. They had never ever quarreled, not once. They were such good friends that they built their houses side by side, with only a path between them.

They had wonderful times together and were so helpful to one another that one of their neighbors became jealous. He was a bit of a wise guy. "I know how to make them quarrel," he said to himself.

This wise guy made himself a coat, red on one side, blue on the other. He walked past the two men as they were busy

in their gardens, stamping loudly all the while. The two men looked up to see who was passing by, then went on with their digging.

"Hey! Did you see that man?" asked one of the friends.

"I did," said the other.

"Did you notice the coat he was wearing?"

"I did," said the other.

"I wish I had a fine red coat like that!"

"Red? But, my friend, that coat was blue."

"Blue? It wasn't blue. It was red."

"No. I am sure it was blue."

"Nonsense. I know it was red."

"Blue!"

"Red!"

"Blue!"

"Idiot!"

"Fool!"

They were so furious with each other that they turned their backs and went on fiercely with their digging.

Then the wise guy walked past again, this time in the other direction, stamping just as loudly as before. The two friends turned round to look.

"You were right, friend, it was a blue coat he was wearing," said one friend to the other.

"No, you were right. It was definitely a red coat. I don't know how I got it wrong."

"No, no. It was blue. I saw it quite clearly this time."

"It was red. I tell you it was red."

"Blue!"

"Red!"

"Blue!"

They were about to come to blows when the wise guy turned around to watch them, forgetting to look where he was going. What a tumble he took, straight into a pile of muck, his coat showing blue on one side and red on the other.

"Look at that wise guy over there," said one of the friends. "He has made great fools of us."

"So he has," said the other friend.

And they sat down and laughed loudly together about the trick that had been played on them. Then they had a drink together to celebrate and make up.

But they didn't invite the wise guy to join them. Oh no. He went to hide his red face!

RHODA RED-HEN

Caroline Pitcher

One fine morning, Rhoda Red-Hen squeezed through the fence into the vegetable garden where she wasn't supposed to go.

"One gets so bored with corn," said Rhoda. "One is looking for something more exciting."

She high-stepped through a forest of broccoli trees and out into the sunlight. A quick scratch with her strong scaly feet uncovered two earthworms, fat as macaroni. Mmmm!

Rhoda stopped, scaly foot poised in mid-scratch.

Someone was watching her.

"Purrrk puk-puk?" called Rhoda. No one answered.

Straight ahead of her was a tepee of bean poles, all twisted over with leaves and red flowers. Perhaps Mrs. Minnings' dog was hiding inside, ready to jump out and chase Rhoda back to the barn?

But all she could see were green beans.

Rhoda cluck-clucked at herself for being silly.

She turned around and *there was the someone!*

The someone was crouching among the pumpkin plants. His big orange face grinned like a jack-o'-lantern on a Halloween night.

"Purrrk puk-puk!" squawked Rhoda when she saw his red tongue lolling, his white teeth gleaming, and his eyes as dark as coals.

Rhoda spread her wings over her head and prayed he would think she was an old feather duster.

"Well, there's a thing!" drawled the fox. "Or should I say, there's a chicken. I come here to sun myself, and what do I find? A naughty old hen."

"Purrrk puk-puk," squawked Rhoda.

"I do wish you'd stop saying that," said the fox. "You didn't expect to find me here, did you?"

"No," said Rhoda.

"Everybody thinks I'm only around when the moon floats in the sky like a silver balloon," sighed the fox. "Now, my dear, how long is it since you laid a splendid brown egg?"

"Er, this morning," said Rhoda.

This was a lie. Rhoda hadn't laid an egg for weeks, and the last one was small, not splendid at all.

"You look a little frazzled, if you don't mind my saying so," said the fox.

"That's because I'm in molt," snapped Rhoda.

The fox gazed at her. His tongue snaked around his lips. "Is there a dog in that house?" he asked casually.

"Yes," squawked Rhoda. "But he's not here when I need him."

"Is he by any chance a foxhound?" asked the fox, examining his sharp nails.

"No, he's a Great Hairy Prannet," said Rhoda.

If the truth be known the dog was a Labrador, not a Great Hairy Prannet. And he was hanging around the oven, because Mrs Minnings was baking chocolate chip cookies

for her grandchildren who were coming that afternoon.

"I think you should come home with me, old hen," whispered the fox.

"I don't," squawked Rhoda.

"Where's your sense of adventure?" he simpered.

"I lost it," said Rhoda. "Wouldn't you like some fresh peas? I'll pop you a pod or two."

"I am not partial to green things, not partial at all," said the fox. "Red is my favorite food color."

"Then let me scratch you up a worm as red as the comb on my head," offered Rhoda.

"I'm weary of worms," yawned the fox.

"A red apple from the orchard?" screeched Rhoda in desperation.

"Perhaps for dessert. But it's a main course I'm after. And I think I've found just the one. Old hen, you have the honor of being destined for dinner. *My* dinner."

Rhoda could not move for fear.

"Some get their chickens from the supermarket, some from the butcher," crooned the fox. "I just happen to like mine *very* fresh."

Now, hens are not especially clever creatures. I mean, you couldn't teach Rhoda to catch a ball in her beak or jump through a flaming hoop. But Rhoda was a plucky hen and she wasn't about to let any old fox get the better of her that easily.

"If red is your favorite food color, sneak into the yard," she suggested. "In the yard there is a chain and at the end of the chain there is a bowl and in the bowl there is some dog meat. It's red."

"Oh yeah?" drawled the fox.

"Oh yeah," squawked Rhoda. "He always leaves a little. Sometimes I have a beakful or two. Meaty chunks with lots of jelly. You wouldn't even have to pluck it. There's turkey flavor, beef flavor, and er..."

"Chicken flavor?" suggested the fox. "They don't sell fox food in cans yet, I suppose. Well, I'll have it by way of a first course."

He crawled toward Rhoda, his belly to the earth. Rhoda saw his teeth shining like carving knives and felt his hot breath.

He whispered, "I know you hens. You won't be able to move for fright. I hypnotize you with my dark eyes . . .

don't move, old hen. I'll be back for the main course soon."

And he slunk away across the grass.

"Purrrk puk-puk," clucked Rhoda. "Here I lie, a chicken take-out. Pull yourself together, hen."

She tried to lift her strong scaly feet. She couldn't move, forward, backward, or sideways.

"How about upward?" squawked Rhoda, and with a great fluttering and flapping she rose into the air and landed on top of the tepee of bean poles, right out of reach of the fox.

But only for a second.

"Get a grip on things, hen," squawked Rhoda, but her feet could not cling on. She toppled and plummeted to the ground.

At that very moment, Mrs. Minnings turned from the oven with a tray of freshly–baked chocolate chip cookies and caught sight through the window of Rhoda plummeting.

"Well if that silly old hen isn't eating my vegetables again!" she cried. And she slammed down the tray of cookies so crossly that they jumped off and rolled into all the corners of the kitchen.

"Now's my chance," barked the Labrador, but Mrs. Minnings pushed him out into the garden and shouted, "Why weren't you doing your job, you Great Hairy Prannet?"

Mrs. Minnings marched across the garden, snatched up Rhoda by her scaly yellow legs, and carried her to the barn.

"How undignified," clucked Rhoda. "Still, better to be upside down than destined for dinner."

"Silly old hen," said Mrs Minnings as she tossed Rhoda into the barn. The old hen righted herself in midair and fluttered up to the top of the hay bales.

In the yard the dog barked, "Phew, I smell fox," and set off on the trail.

In the vegetable garden, the fox said, "Now's my chance. Where's my dinner? Yoo-hoo! Where are you, my dear?"

"Here!" snarled the dog, leaping out from behind the pumpkins, and he chased that fox over hills and down dales and right into his den.

In the barn, Rhoda Red-Hen decided she hadn't had such a dreadful day since the time she gobbled up hailstones thinking they were henfood from heaven.

"One will just settle for corn tomorrow," she clucked as she settled down to sleep.

THE BRIC-A-BRACS

Joyce Dunbar

Maisie saw the dollhouse first, on the white elephant stand at the school fair.

"I like that," she said.

"It's falling to pieces," said her mother.

"I still like it," said Maisie.

"It's more trouble than it's worth," said her mother.

But Maisie had enough allowance of her own saved up so she bought the dollhouse and carried it home.

She set it down, opened up the front, and started to sweep out the rooms.

Then she heard a tiny tap-tapping in the attic.

She lifted the front flap of the roof.

What a mess she found. There were broken bits of furniture, scraps of fabric, empty spools of thread, matchboxes, string, and huddled in the middle of it all —

"Mr. Bric-a-Brac," announced a pipe cleaner man, holding out a pipe cleaner hand.

"Mrs. Bric-a-Brac," said a pipe cleaner woman, dusting herself down. "Did you ever see such a mess! Are you the new help?"

"I think so," said Maisie.

"Then we'd better get started," said Mrs. Bric-a-Brac briskly. "Can you believe it? Swept out of the house! Bundled into the attic! Jiggled and joggled about! Where's Baby Bric-a-Brac? Where's Ric-Rac? Where's everything? Come on. We'd better get our sleeves rolled up."

So Maisie got her sleeves rolled up.

She searched until she found baby Bric-a-Brac, tucked up tight inside a matchbox, and she gave her to Mrs. Bric-a-Brac. Then she found Ric-Rac, a pipe cleaner dog with a curly tail and she gave him to Mr. Bric-a-Brac.

"You can see we've got our hands full now," said Mrs. Bric-a-Brac to Maisie. "So you'll have to sort out the house. Never mind. I'll tell you what to do. Dear oh dear. I don't think we'll ever get straight."

"We will," said Maisie. "You'll see."

Maisie worked very hard. She swept, cleaned, polished, mended. She put down rugs and pinned up drapes. She put the matchbox beds in the bedroom with the matchbox chest of drawers. She put the margarine tub table in the kitchen with the spools as stools. Mrs.

Bric-a-Brac bossed and fussed, trying to make sure that everything was put in its right place. Mr. Bric-a-Brac came back from a run with Ric-Rac, then helped Maisie decide where to put the postage stamp pictures. At the end of the day they were nearly straight.

"That's much better," sighed Mrs. Bric-a-Brac. "It's beginning to feel like home again."

"We'll be able to sleep in our own beds tonight," said Mr. Bric-a-Brac.

"I'll make you some new things tomorrow," said Maisie. "And we can do a little decorating."

"That will be wonderful," said Mrs. Bric-a-Brac. "Now, I wonder what's for supper?"

A week later, over supper, Maisie's mother was talking to Maisie's father. "Maisie really loves that battered old dollhouse," she said. "She's spent all week collecting odds and ends to make things for it. She's going to stay with her grandmother soon. Why don't we fix it up as a surprise for when she returns?"

"That's an idea," said her father.

When Maisie returned from her grandmother's, she went straight to her room to show the Bric-a-Bracs the dog basket and television set she had made for them. The dollhouse was covered with a sheet. Maisie pulled it off.

The dollhouse had been freshly painted. It had a new door with a letter box and a chimney on the roof. All the rooms were papered, each with a different pattern. It was furnished from wall to wall with everything that a doll-

house ought to have. Maisie was silent for a while, trying to understand.

"Where are the things that were in it?" she asked at last.

"In the cardboard box," said her mother.

Maisie rummaged in the box. She found Mr. and Mrs. Bric-a-Brac and the baby and Ric-Rac. She showed them round the dollhouse, but they didn't say a word. She walked them up and down the stairs, but they didn't smile at all. She sat them at the new table on the new chairs, and they stayed there, perfectly still. Ric-Rac didn't even wag his tail.

"Let's see how Maisie's getting on with her dollhouse," said Maisie's mother to Maisie's father, later on that day. They opened her door just a crack, and peeped inside.

There, in empty splendor, stood the dollhouse. With her back to it sat Maisie, a pair of scissors in one hand, the cardboard box in the other. She had cut out a door and two windows. She seemed to be talking to herself.

"I *know* you were just getting settled. I *know* you liked it the way it was. But I'm making you a new house, see? You can use all your own furniture and you can choose your own colors for the walls."

"Dear oh dear," said Mrs. Bric-a-Brac, "I don't think we'll ever get straight."

"We will," said Maisie. "You'll see."

TOM THUMB

Traditional

A woodcutter was chopping logs in his yard while his wife threw corn to the chickens. "If only we had a child to play around us," he said, "then we should be really happy."

"I couldn't agree more," said his wife. "Why, if I could have one small son, even no bigger than my thumb, I should be the happiest woman alive."

Now it so happened that the fairies heard them and decided to grant their wish. Not long after, the woodcutter's wife had a tiny child, not much bigger than her thumb. He could walk and talk in no time, and the fairies made him a suit of clothes. His hat was made of an oak leaf, his shirt spun out of spiderwebs, his jacket woven from thistledown, and his pants from feathers.

His mother and father were overjoyed. "We have got what we wished for," they said, "and we will always love him dearly." They called him Tom Thumb.

Even though he was so little, he was as merry and mischievous as any child could be. "Can I help you plow the fields, father?" he asked one day.

"Why no, you are much too small to ride a horse, Tom," said his father.

"Oh no I'm not," said Tom. "Just set me in the horse's ear." His father did so. "Whoa," said Tom, and "Steady," straight into the horse's ear. All went well until Tom decided to go for a gallop. "Gee-up!" he suddenly yelled, so that the horse ran through the town, upsetting all the market stalls in the street.

"You are a bad lad, Tom Thumb," said his father when he caught up with him. "You will never make your way in

the world if you play tricks like that."

Even so, he let Tom ride home in his favorite place on the rim of his hat, for his son was the apple of his eye.

"Can I help you mix the batter pudding?" Tom asked his mother on another day.

"But, Tom, you are too small," she replied.

"Oh no, I'm not," said Tom. "Just set me on the table."

But no sooner was her back turned than Tom decided to go boating on the bowl of batter in half an eggshell.

The eggshell upturned, tipping Tom Thumb into the mixture. He kicked and thrashed around, and might have drowned if his mother hadn't fished him out in time.

"Whatever shall I do with you?" she said. "I don't see how you will ever make your way in the world."

Even so, she kissed him and washed him in a teacup, for her son was her pride and joy.

Soon after, Tom's mother took him out milking in the meadow. He sneaked out of her apron pocket and ran down a snail shell. "Here I am!" he called. Then he hid down a mouse hole. "Here I am," he called. Then he crept under a stone, still calling, "Here I am."

This time his mother caught him and tied him to a thistle with a fine thread so that she might get on with her milking. But the cow thought she saw a tasty morsel and took Tom and the thistle in one mouthful. Round and round he was tumbled, with the cow's great teeth chewing and grinding. "Here I am, mother!" he cried out in terror.

"You're a wicked little boy, Tom Thumb," she replied. "I cannot play hide-and-seek all morning." And she went on with her milking.

"Mother, please come and get me!" yelled Tom, so loudly

that his voice tickled the cow's tonsils and he was coughed up into the long grass. He began waving his arms so wildly that a raven swept him up and dropped him into the sea, where he was swallowed by an enormous fish.

Luckily, the fish was caught soon after and presented to a king for his supper. What a shock everyone got when out popped Tom Thumb.

The king was delighted with him. He gave him a mouse with a saddle to ride on, and a darning needle for a sword. Tom charged around, scaring spiders away from the three princesses, so that they made him their champion knight.

But Tom was missing his father and mother. "You shall go home to see them," said the king, "and you shall take all the treasure you can carry."

They made him a golden coach from a walnut shell, with

four silver buttons for wheels and six mice to pull it.

Tom set off home with all his treasure, which was a single gold coin. But it took him all day just to reach the edge of the palace grounds. "Don't worry," said the princesses. "We have some presents from the fairies that will help you to find your way home."

The first princess gave him an enchanted hat, which shrank to fit the wearer's head, and showed him whatever was going on in all parts of the world. The second gave him a pair of boots, which shrank to fit the wearer's feet, and could in a moment carry him to all corners of the earth. The third gave him a precious ring, which he wore around his waist like a girdle and which gave him the strength of a giant.

Tom Thumb put on the hat and saw his mother and father weeping for the loss of him. So he put on the boots and wished that he was home.

"Here I am, mother," he cried. "See, father! I *have* made my way in the world!"

And to show he had the strength of a giant, he lifted them up in his arms before giving them a great big hug!